Queenie Pugweenie

By
John Alexander Lott

Illustrated by
Nathan Gevenois

DEDICATION

To Jenn, who brought a four-legged wonder into our lives, and to Charly the Pugweenie, my inspiration for this book.

On a day clean and bright, all fresh and all springy,

Mommy came home with a puppy all clingy.

Her fur was
light brown and
her tail was so
curly.

She was proper and prim, in a manner quite girly.

The way that she pranced and danced cross the floor,

Made Daddy laugh as he walked through the door.

With a scrunched up wet nose,

and her chin in the air,

She made it her job to inspect

everyone there.

Her whimper was quiet. A howl just wouldn't do.

Someone was special, and she'd let you know who.

With puppy dog eyes that would make sadness flee,

It was easy to see she was pure royalty.

Her family decided the
name "Queenie" was best.
She liked it and soon put
her name to the test.

She would turn up her nose if food wasn't just right.

She'd whine and she'd whimper long into the night.

When friends came to play, she would make
not a peep,
Just turn herself round and go right to sleep.

Though quite small in stature, she tried very hard,

To scowl and look down upon things in the yard.

There lived in the house, that was right next door,

A terrifying creature, called "Black Labrador."

He made such a ruckus, and shook the whole fence,

That Queenie decided to give him her two cents.

She told him where to go, and just how to get there.

And, when she could, finish off with a glare.

On the opposite side of the house from the creature,

Prowled many great beasts, all with the same feature.

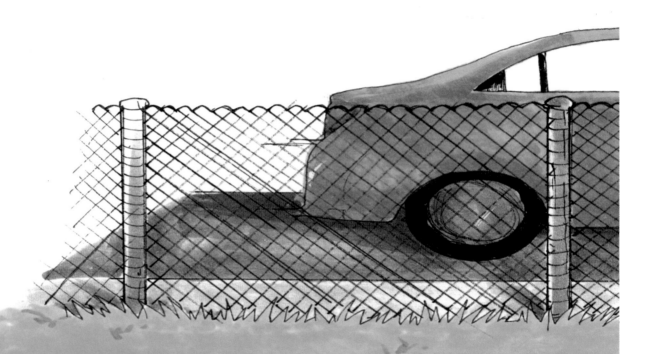

They were shiny and each of them had in their belly,

A person, just sitting. And boy, were they smelly!

She could smell them for miles, as they passed
from her sight,
And they kept going by through the day and
the night.

She yipped and she barked and said things very rude.

It made other dogs think, she had a bad attitude.

Then one day another dog stopped to say "Hi."
Queenie thought he was trouble from the look in
his eye.

His fur was all scruffy, and he was
just Queenie's size.

But it turned out this dog was someone quite wise.

"My name is Buddy. And I'd like to play."

"The Queen has no need of such things on this day."

Buddy's smile went away, but still he persisted.

He did flips and roll-overs 'til his body was twisted.

"Even a Queen should have fun every day.

I think that you'll like it if you come out to play."

"For how can you rule, if you don't know your subjects?

You'll see playing is something to which nobody objects."

"You will make lots of friends as you open up.

And treat others with kindness as a true royal pup."

And so Queenie thought, "Hey, this dog's not so bad.

A Queen in her castle can get lonely and sad."

"But I've been so mean and so rude to the others,

I must make it right with my sisters and brothers."

Buddy smiled as he said with a twinkle in his eye.

"I think they'll forgive you if you let them try."

So a valuable lesson was learned by our Queenie.

That being a Queen meant *not* being a meanie.

She made friends with the Lab, and stopped chasing beasts.

And with all her friends, had fantastical feasts.

A ruler and friend unto all, huge or teeny.

Thus started her reign, as Queenie Pugweenie.

Made in the USA
Las Vegas, NV
18 February 2021